Helena Pielichaty (pronounced Pierre-li-hatty) has written numerous books for children, including *Simone's Letters*, which was nominated for the Carnegie Medal, and the popular After School Club series. A long-standing Huddersfield Town supporter, there are few who could write with as much enthusiasm about girls' football. A love of the game clearly runs in the family: her aunt was in a women's team in the 1950s and her daughter played football from the age of ten to twenty-six. Helena lives in Nottinghamshire with her husband and has two grown-up children.

Do Goalkeepers Wear Tiaras?

Can Ponies Take Penalties?

Are all Brothers Foul?

Is an own Goal Bad?

Who Ate all the Pies?

What's Ukrainian for Football?

So What If I Hog the Ball?

Can't I Just Kick It?

We're the Dream Team, Right?

Has Anyone Seen our Striker?

Do Shinpads Come in Pink?

Do Shinpads Come in Pink?

Helena Pielichaty

WALKER
BOOKS

For my son, Joe – in a league

of his own since 1987

First published 2012 by Walker Books Ltd
87 Vauxhall Walk, London SE11 5HJ

10 9 8 7 6 5 4 3 2 1

Text © 2012 Helena Pielichaty
Cover illustration © 2012 Sonia Leong

The right of Helena Pielichaty to be identified as author
of this work has been asserted by her in accordance with
the Copyright, Designs and Patents Act 1988

This book has been typeset in Helvetica and Handwriter

Printed and bound in Great Britain by Clays Ltd, St Ives plc

British Library Cataloguing in Publication Data:
a catalogue record for this book is available from the British Library

ISBN 978-1-4063-1732-9

www.walker.co.uk

☆ ☆ The Team ☆ ☆

☆ **Megan "Meggo" Fawcett** GOAL

☆ **Petra "Wardy" Ward** DEFENCE

☆ **Lucy "Goose" Skidmore** DEFENCE

☆ **Dylan "Dyl" or "Psycho 1" McNeil** LEFT WING

☆ **Holly "Hols" or "Wonder" Woolcock** DEFENCE

☆ **Veronika "Nika" Kozak** MIDFIELD

☆ **Jenny-Jane "JJ" or "Hoggy" Bayliss** MIDFIELD

☆ **Gemma "Hursty" Hurst** MIDFIELD

☆ **Eve "Akky" Akboh** STRIKER

☆ **Tabinda "Tabby" or "Tabs" Shah** STRIKER/MIDFIELD

☆ **Daisy "Dayz" or "Psycho 2" McNeil** RIGHT WING

☆ **Amy "Minto" or "Lil Posh" Minter** VARIOUS

Official name: Parrs Under 11s, also known as the Parsnips

Ground: Lornton FC, Low Road, Lornton

Capacity: 500

Affiliated to: the Nettie Honeyball Women's League
junior division

Sponsors: Sweet Peas Garden Centre, Mowborough

Club colours: red and white; red shirts with white sleeves,
white shorts, red socks with white trim

Coach: Hannah Preston

Assistant coach: Katie Regan

☆ ☆ Star Player ☆ ☆

☆ **Age:** 11

☆ **School:** St Mary's Prep but by the time you read this I'll probably be at St Agatha's Girls' High School (Saggies)

☆ **Position in team:** see Pre-match Interview

☆ **Likes:** magazine competitions, fashion news, parties, hanging out with friends, Spanish food

☆ **Dislikes:** freaky-shaped vegetables, gum (and worse) on your shoes, school dinners

☆ **Supports:** What? Like a football team? Nooooooooooooooooooo.

☆ **Favourite player(s) on team:** Gemma Hurst (BFF) Holly Woolcock (BFF #2)

☆ **Best football moment:** when Gemma came back to the Parrs.

Amy "Minto" Minter

☆ **Match preparation:** Top tip — sun protection (factor 30)

☆ **Have you got a lucky mascot or a ritual you have to do before or after a match?**
Nope. I leave that kind of things to the jockettes.

☆ **What do you do in your spare time?**
Plan my interview for **Junior Apprentice**. Please let it still be airing by the time I'm sixteen. I'll walk it.

☆ **Favourite book(s):** It was **Twilight** but I'm so over the whole Bella and Edward thing now. Reading **Shout**, **Mizz** and **Bliss** until I decide.

☆ **Favourite band(s):** anything from Ella Fitzgerald to Taylor Swift

☆ **Favourite film:** The Devil Wears Prada

☆ **Favourite TV programme(s):** Junior Apprentice, Glee, Miranda, Project Catwalk

Hola, Sweetpeas. My name is Amy Minter and I am the striker-midfield-defender-whatever for the Parrs Under 11s. In other words I'm so useless I don't have a particular position. What can I say? Some of us were born to hit the crossbar, some of us were born to hit the nail bar.

I'm here to tell you what happened at the end of the second season. To be honest, there's only the presentation evening left. I think Megan was terrified I'd mess up if she let me loose on actual football stuff, what with all my heinous girly ways. LOL! But don't worry. I'm going to prove I can deliver a soccer story that'll blow all the others out of the changing rooms.

Just give me five to brush my hair
first, OK? XOXO

Amy

B.T.W. I'm presenting my series of
unfortunate events to you magazine-
stylee. Hope u like…

1

Let's Begin with Some FUN FACTS

Fact 1: We finished fourth in the league this season. That's out of ten teams. I think it's the perfect place. Like, not so high as to be saying "look at me" and not low enough to be shouting for help.

Fact 2: We won the Nettie Honeyball Cup. Yay! I'm not exaggerating when I tell you that the cup final could be made into a film. Seriously. I'd love to tell you more about it but Megan's like: *"Eve covered the whole thing in her section. It's yesterday's news."* Yeah, right! I've heard Megan has polished that "yesterday's news" cup so often people have to wear shades when they pass by.

Fact 3: Six of the squad will be leaving. They are:

- ☆ Gemma Hurst (my BFF, super-talented but modest with it. Keeps things close to her chest)

- ☆ Eve Akboh (top striker and fun to be with once you get to know her)

- ☆ Holly Woolcock (defender and all-round good egg)

- ☆ Lucy Skidmore (defender, cool, calm and collected)

- ☆ Nika Kozak (midfield, a sensitive person with really peachy skin)

- ☆ *Petite Moi* (your style correspondent)

Fact 4: Six of the squad will be staying on:

- ☆ Megan Fawcett (captain, focused and organized but maybe a bit obsessed with the whole football thing)

- ☆ Petra Ward (defender and Megan's quiet sidekick. Loyal with a capital *L*)

- ☆ Tabinda Shah (midfield, gorge long black

hair and thick eyelashes)

- ☆ Daisy and Dylan McNeil (kooky identical twins, hilarious off and on the pitch)
- ☆ Jenny-Jane Bayliss (my least fave member of the team. I mean, would it hurt her to crack a smile now and again?)

F.Y.I. We aren't leaving because there was a major rift or anything; we just got too old. *Too old*. All my life I've been *too young* for things: liquid eyeliner, Jimmy Choos, my own Facebook page – the list is *endless*. To be told I'm too old for something is pretty radical.

Fact 5: Hannah Preston (22) and Katie Regan (20), our ace coaches, are also leaving. Hannah's going to teacher-training college and Katie's backpacking round Oz with her BFF. It's a blow for girls' football, is all I can say. That pair ooze inspiration. The fact that I stuck it out as a Parr for two whole seasons when I sucked at football is proof of that.

Fact 6: There are only twenty-two days to go before the presentation evening. Eek! In case you don't know, a presentation evening is like a party for footballers. It's held at the end of the season to celebrate all your achievements, and afterwards, instead of party bags to take home, you get trophies and medals. The outstanding players get bigger trophies and medals such as "Player of the Year". For players like me who are not to be weighed down by such heavy-duty booty, it's all about the dancing, the food, the games and the mingling with your mates. This year, with so many of us leaving, a few of us have decided the presentation evening should be bigger and better than ever before and we've formed ... a committee (see Fact 7).

Fact 7: The presentation evening committee. I'm on it along with Gemma, Eve and Holly. Our role originally was just to collect money for Hannah and Katie's presents, but after five seconds it was obvious to me that we couldn't stop there. No way were we going to simply rock up with a bunch of flowers and a box of Sensations on my watch. Our cool coaches deserve more than that. We've got big plans, people. Check out this list of things that need sorting:

Venue/decoration of
Catering
Presents 4 H & K
Speeches
Entertainment

If I tell you each of those main headings has got about twenty sub-headings to go with it, you'll know where I'm coming from. The pressure is on.

Tomorrow morning Gemma and I are going to meet Megan's auntie Mandy, who runs the clubhouse where we're having the do, to go over the list with her. I can't wait.

And that's the intro, girlfriends. Ready for some drama?

DID I SAY DRAMA?

I meant background information. Don't wanna over-excite you toooooooooooooo soon, do I?

Let me set the scene for you. I'll start the day before the meeting with Mandy when Mum picked me up from after-school club. She was frazzled, and late, because some delivery guy had shown up just as she was closing her shop. It didn't help that the shop, Tom and Betty's "cute couture for cute kids" is on the Parade on the far side of town, so it meant she'd hit all the rush-hour traffic. My mum is not good in rush-hour traffic. Anything below thirty miles an hour is not her style. "... Not only that," she told me, "but it wasn't even my order. Before I had a chance to say anything, he'd dumped ten boxes of XXL T-shirts on the floor and skedaddled."

"Where will you put them?" I asked, fearing the worst. Since Mum converted the ground-floor storeroom into an office, my bedroom (we live in a flat above the shop) seems to have become a magnet for surplus stock. I wouldn't mind if any of it actually fitted me but I'm way beyond the three- to four-year age range. LOL!

Mum sighed. "Look behind you."

I turned. The back seat was rammed with brown boxes. "I thought there was no point carting them up the stairs only to bring them back down again on Monday when they collect them."

"*If* they collect them," I said.

"They'd better!" She laughed. "Let's get home and have something to eat."

That was music to my ears. I was absolutely starving. "Let's eat at Miro's. It'll save you cooking."

Miro's is the tapas bar only two doors down from Mum's shop, and Carlos and Rosa, who run it, are so sweet. They're like the grandparents I never had, only more Spanish.

"No. We're eating there tomorrow..."

"Are we? Since when?"

"Shane's taking us."

That got my attention. The deal with Mum's boyfriends is I only meet the serious ones and I hadn't realized Shane, who she's been seeing for a couple of months, had been promoted. "OK, give me the deets so I can prepare."

"I'm not giving you any 'deets'. You'll only start picking faults."

"That means you're hiding stuff. Please tell me he's not married."

"No."

"Newly divorced with a really bitter wife?"

"No."

"A single dad with three brats who'll hate me on sight?"

"No."

"He wears capri shorts even though he's in his thirties?"

"No!"

I relaxed. Those, in order, are my top four worst-case scenarios. Anything else I can handle.

Two minutes later, we arrived home. Some people find it weird that I live above a shop but I love it. The Parade is opposite the botanical gardens and the views from my bedroom are gorge. Not that I had much viewing time that day. I'd barely stepped out of my school kilt when Gemma called, apologizing like crazy because her dad wouldn't be able to take us to the clubhouse in the morning. Apparently her big sis, Lizzie, and friends needed a lift to the station. "He says we could reschedule for the afternoon instead?"

I groaned. "But Mandy only had that slot. She has to get the bar ready for opening from eleven."

"Well, what if you get someone to drop you off and we pick you up?"

"Like who? My mum can't. Saturday's her busiest day."

"Megan's dad maybe? Isn't Megan going anyway because her mum and dad are working?"

"But I don't want to go with Megan and her dad. I want to go with you. It was all planned."

"What shall we do, then? Leave it until next week?"

I knew we didn't have time to postpone. There was way too much to do. "I'll call Megan." I sighed and hung up.

As usual Megan was sooooooooooo sweet with me. "I guess Dad could pick you up," she grunted after I'd explained. "Though we weren't planning on setting off that early. We'll be picking Petra up too."

"Fine."

"I still don't get why you need to look round. You've seen the place a million times."

"Not as project manager I haven't."

"Project manager? Oh, give me a break."

I didn't say anything. I was trying not to let her

attitude get to me. Never once has she said "Thanks for doing this, Amy. I really appreciate all the hours you've put into organizing the presentation evening," or: "That's a good idea, Amy."

"Will you need a lift back?" she asked. When I told her I was OK because Gemma's dad was picking me up, her whole attitude changed. "What time? Will Gemma hang around for a while? Do you think she'd have a kick-about?"

"I doubt it," I said, thinking we'd need to get straight back.

Monotone Meg returned instantly. "Oh," she said. "See you at half-nine, then."

I said thank you and hung up, trying not to reel from all that enthusiasm.

3

Fall Out in the Function Room

Next morning, Mandy Leggitt was waiting for us in the clubhouse lounge. She was dressed in jeans and a washed-out sweatshirt with the name of a beer company flashed all over it, and immediately launched into an incomprehensible conversation with Megan and Megan's dad about something called play-offs.

They banged on about them for at least five minutes. Petra listened politely but I was like, *Hello, I hope this isn't eating into my consultation period.* Luckily, Auntie M. caught my eye. "I see someone's come prepared," she said, smiling at my clipboard with its tape measure attachment.

Finally! "I was hoping we could start by checking the dimensions of the stage area," I said.

For some reason she found that amusing. "Stage area's a bit of a grand title for it but feel free. You know your way, don't you?"

This was puzzling. "Aren't you coming too? I've got a lot of questions I need to ask." Forty-seven, to be precise.

"Me? Oh no, m'duck. I've got the bar to get ready. I'll leave you with our Megs; she's the boss today." She winked at her niece. Why did I get the impression I wasn't being taken seriously?

I followed Megan and Petra upstairs. "Here you go. Knock yourself out," Megan said as she pushed open the double doors to the function room.

I can describe it to you in two words. Beyond dismal. Bringing a funky feel to this place was going to be a real challenge. "We'll be able to rearrange the tables on the night, won't we?" I asked.

Megan shrugged. "I suppose so. Why?"

"To give more space for the entertainment."

"What entertainment?"

I hesitated at first, not sure how much the committee would want me to give away just yet but then I thought, Why not? I knew Megan and Petra wouldn't tell Hannah and Katie. "We've got this amazing dance act from Eve's church called the Jump-leads..."

Someone behind me snorted. I turned to see JJ standing in the doorway. I should have guessed she'd muscle in at some point. She often meets Megan here on Saturdays.

She started criticizing immediately. "A dance act? What? In pink sparkly tutus?" she sneered and did what I supposed was meant to be a pirouette.

I scowled at her. I would not let myself be wound up by that pain today. "Actually no, they're more—"

"Wait, Amy, just wait," Megan interrupted before the words "hip" or "hop" could leave my thwarted little throat. She nodded towards Petra and JJ. "Can you give us a minute?"

"Thank you so much," I said after they'd gone. "I don't mind Petra but JJ just presses all the wrong buttons."

Megan ran her hand through her hair. "This is nuts."

"Nuts?"

"Yes. N.U.T.S. Nuts. All this dance act and measuring stuff. Why can't it be like last year? A few sausages on sticks and everybody having a laugh? You don't need to complicate it."

"Hello? How is this complicated? All you'll have to do is turn up! Anyway, don't you want to give Hannah and Katie a big send-off? I know I do."

As soon as I said that the temperature plummeted to minus thirty. Megan gave me a cold, hard stare. "I'm going to the field to have a kick-around. Drop the latch when you're done, OK?" Then she turned and left the room.

Un-be-lievable. If she felt like this why had she let me come in the first place? Honestly! Just wait until I reported this to the committee on Monday.

I looked round, thinking I might start measuring

up, but the idea of staying in such a miserable dump on my own gave me the heebie-jeebies. Instead I went outside, found a bench and spent the rest of the time checking out fashion goss on my Trendtracker app.

After what felt like four centuries, Gemma's dad's car pulled up. I cannot tell you what a relief that was. Of course, the second Gemma's foot touched gravel the three amigos were over her like a rash. "Aw, go on, Gem. Just a quick game," Megan begged.

"Footy? I thought this was meant to be a business meeting?" Gemma laughed as Petra and JJ tried dragging her onto the pitch. She glanced over her shoulder at me but I just gave a little shrug. Much as I wanted to go home I would never try to stop Gemma playing football. It would be like snatching the microphone away from Taylor Swift. A crime against nature.

Gemma looked longingly at the goalmouth, then sighed. "I can't. We've got to get back to take the dogs out. Maybe when we come to rehearse the presentation evening we can slip a game in?"

"Rehearse?" Megan asked.

"The Jump-leads..."

"Oh, that's not happening. Megan thinks a dance act will complicate things," I explained, trying not to sound miffed, and failing.

Megan dug her hands into her jeans pocket. "Well, I thought it might but if you think it's a good idea, Gem, maybe we should go for it..."

"Yes, let's," Petra agreed immediately.

My heart began pounding faster than a fan's outside Justin Beiber's dressing-room door. So that was the score, was it? When I came up with a suggestion it was "taking things too seriously", but when Gemma said it... Well, that did it. That was the final straw. I'd put up with so much flak since joining the Parrs. The eye-rolling if I didn't take the game one hundred per cent seriously. The snide comments from Jenny-Jane if I dared to say anything remotely girly. Now this. All my input shoved aside without a second's thought. Well, fine.

They could take their sausages on sticks and shove them up their noses for all I cared.

Without another word, I turned and marched off. I didn't even stop at the car. I just kept going down the drive and out onto the road. In fact, I had almost reached the end of the village before Gemma's dad pulled his car up alongside me. "OK, speedy Gonzales. Hop in." He laughed.

In the car, Gemma did her best to calm me down but I was too worked up to listen. "It's all right for you," I said. "Megan thinks you walk on water. I'm just the one who tags along and gets insulted every week."

"Amy that's not true."

But it was true and we both knew it.

4

Later that Day ... when I'd had time to calm down a teeny-tiny bit (but not that much) ...

Came ... THE DATE

"OK. How do I look? Marks out of ten?"
Mum revolved slowly on her high heels and splayed the pleats of her dress so I could see the snazzy netting of her underskirt underneath.

"Ten."

"You're sure? What about the polka-dot scarf? Or the patent belt? Too much?"

"Mum, you look gorge."

"Aw, thanks, babe. What about you? What are you going to wear?"

"Hello!" I said, holding my hands out to show I was ready.

She looked surprised that I was still in my blue cut-offs and the white puff-sleeved top I'd had on all day, but we were running late so that saved me having to explain why I hadn't felt like getting changed.

Still, despite running late we weren't as late as Shane. When we arrived at Miro's he was nowhere to be seen. Way to make a first impression! Carlos, his brown, bald head shining with perspiration, greeted us like he always does with effusive pecks on both cheeks. "Debbie! Amy! *Cóma está usted?* How are you? Long time no see."

"We're good, thanks. We're good," Mum replied, as I waved at Rosa, who waved back and blew a kiss at me.

Carlos showed us to our usual table, holding out the chair for Mum. "Now, what can I get you? The early-bird menu has finished but for my special guests I make exception."

"Can you give us a minute, babe? We're waiting for someone," Mum told him.

"Shane," I said. "And he's late."

Carlos tutted. "Late? For you? Inexcusable. I will spit in his soup!" He took our drinks order and went away chuckling.

Mum asked how I'd got on at the club but I just said, "Fine."

"You don't sound fine."

I took a deep breath. "Well," I began, but her eyes were fixed somewhere over my shoulder and I knew the moment had gone.

"Oh, here's Shane..." she cooed and I turned to see this guy walking towards us. There were two immediate minuses added to the one for being late – the slate-grey capri shorts and the harassed look on his face. "Debs, I'm so sorry..."

OK, make that three minuses. Mum is *Debbie*.

"No worries," she said. "We've been chatting away."

He looked at me and smiled apologetically. "Amy! Hey!" He held out his hand for me to shake.

"Hi," I said.

"Aren't you going to sit down?" Mum asked, batting her eyelashes.

"I'd love to but ... um ... bit of a domestic."

Uh-oh, I thought. This has got to be an ex-issue.

As it turned out it wasn't his ex-issue it was his sister Kay's ex-issue. Her ex-husband hadn't turned up to collect their son, Shane's thirteen-year-old nephew, Ashley. "... And Kay's had this thing in London booked for months, so I said I'd look after him. I'm so sorry..." His voice petered out.

"Where is he now?" Mum asked.

"In the car, refusing to budge. It's the second time this month his dad's let him down and he's pretty cut up about it. I think it's best if I just head home. I'm sorry." He turned to me. "Maybe some other time, huh? I need serious words with you about Debs's taste in music..." This from the guy in capri pants – but I took his point.

I glanced across at Mum. She looked so crestfallen and Shane did seem quite a nice guy.

"Shall I go and talk to Ashley?" I offered.

"I don't know. He's in a bit of a mood," Shane said.

"Let her try," Mum told him. "They've got a lot in common. Amy's got a deadbeat dad too."

"Mum!"

"Well, it's true."

"You are so embarrassing."

But it was Shane, not Mum, who looked embarrassed. "I'd better head off. I'll call you later, Debs." He kissed Mum on the cheek and left.

Mum watched him go, sighing heavily. It looked like neither of us was having a good day.

5

What Happens in the Gazebo
Stays in the Gazebo

An Amy Minter Confidential

Have you heard that song "I don't like Mondays"? Well, I so agree with whoever wrote it. I don't like Mondays either. Mondays mean Miss Sturgeon all day and she does my head in. Then it's two more hours of after-school club and that does my head in too. Having to trail from my school, St Mary's, all the way across town to Mowborough Primary to get to it doesn't help. Worst of all, when we do get there there's nothing to do – unless you love PlayDoh.

That's why Operation Present 4 Hannah and Katie has been such a blast. I've loved coming up with all the ideas and filling in spreadsheets and stuff. It's given me a sense of purpose. I don't mean just at after-school club but on the team, too. It felt like what I was doing counted for something for once. So when Megan threw it all back in my face on Saturday I was gutted because it meant my time on the committee was over. I was resigning the second I walked through that after-school-club door at four o'clock.

"Oh, don't be like that," Gemma pleaded as we stepped down from the minibus.

"Like what?"

"In a hump. I'm sure Megan didn't mean to upset you."

"Oh, please. She hates me."

"She does not hate you. She just takes football really, really seriously."

"So do I."

"No offence but since when?"

"What about that time I played in the pouring rain with no thought whatsoever for how frizzy my hair would get?"

"Amy, you came on carrying an umbrella."

"So?"

Gemma grinned and leapt up the clubhouse steps. "Idiot."

"Name-calling is so bad for my self-esteem. I've got a good mind to..." "Report you" I was going to say until I spotted Megan and Petra standing by Mrs Rose's desk. I frowned. What were they doing here?

Eve was with them, talking for Britain as usual. "You've got visitors. Isn't that nice?" Mrs Rose, the supervisor, announced when she saw me staring.

I ignored her and turned to Eve. "Where's Holly?"

"Gazebo."

Without another word, I headed outside, not even stopping to check if Gemma was following. She could look after our visitors if she wanted to. I felt no such obligation.

In the gazebo, Holly hitched up so I could sit next to her. "Have you seen Megan and Petra?" she asked.

"Unfortunately."

"What do you mean?"

"I'll tell you later. What's new?"

"Well..." she began but wasn't given a chance to finish.

"Budge up, dudes," Eve ordered as she ushered Petra and Megan into the shelter. Gemma sat down last, squashing in between me and Holly.

I admit I had been intending to blank Megan for the duration but she did something so unexpected I had to change my mind. She apologized. "I was out of order on Saturday, Amy. I'm really sorry. It's just that when you said you wanted to give Hannah and Katie a big send-off, it sounded like you thought I didn't."

"Oh no," I said. "That wasn't what I meant at all."

"I know. I guess I'm not used to you being the one on the team that organizes things. No offence."

"None taken." My shoulders relaxed and the anger that had built up since Saturday seeped away. Megan had *apologized*. For the first time *ever*.

"You'll still get the Jump-leads, won't you?" Petra asked.

"Can't," Eve told her. "They backed out. I was going to tell you all today..."

"No probs. We'll find something else. I have a thousand options," I said, feeling all happy and bouncy and project manager-y again. Me? Resign? No way José.

I plunged into my bag for the minute book, where we recorded everything for the presentation evening. Now we were all chummy again it seemed only fair to share what we'd planned so far. Unfortunately, I have the world's biggest school bag and couldn't find the book anywhere among my piles of stuff. "OK, talk among yourselves, people. Organization fail..."

Holly filled in. "What kind of music shall we go for? A party's not a party without music."

"And a chocolate fountain. That's a must," Eve added.

"Found it!" I said, pulling out the green ledger and flicking through the pages. "OK, here goes..." I began then stopped. There was a deathly hush. All eyes were fixed on Megan, whose head was now bowed.

"Are we saying grace?" I asked but Gemma shot me a warning look. Then, out of nowhere – well, out of Megan actually – came the most horrendous sobs.

The sobs became louder and louder even as Petra wrapped her arm round her best friend's shoulder. "I shouldn't have mentioned the dancing." She sighed.

"Why not?"

"Because it just rubs it in, doesn't it?"

"Rubs what in?"

"Look. It's all right for you lot. The presentation evening's like a big jolly party but for those of us left behind it's the end."

"Why is it the end?" Gemma whispered, addressing Megan's mop of curly hair. "I know it's hard to say goodbye to Hannah and Katie but you've got a new coach lined up, haven't you? I thought Sian was taking over? From the seniors? So it's only the end for us, not you."

Megan's head shot up; her face glistening with tears. "But without you it is the end for us, you dweeb!"

The look of astonishment on Gemma's face was classic. "Me?"

"Of course you! You're awesome! You and Eve both are. There'll never be another pair who link up so brilliantly, will there? There'll never be another Dream Team. Or another midfielder with Nika's quick thinking or another two as brave as Holly and Lucy at the back. You're all unique. You're all so ace..." Megan's face crumpled again and then, without another word, she jumped up from the bench and hurried off.

"What she's trying to say is she'll miss you guys

as much as she'll miss Han and Katie. She thinks the new team's going to be rubbish without you in it. We all do," Petra told us, her eyes full of tears too as she raced off after Megan.

There was a long pause.

"Well, I didn't see that one coming!" Eve said.

6

Find Out What Amy Does for the First Time EVER!!

An Amy Minter Exclusive!

"You all right, babe?" Mum said later that evening.

We were sitting on the sofa watching TV, waiting for our nail varnish to dry.

"Of course I'm all right. Why?"

"You've been so quiet all evening."

"Oh, just some stuff on my mind."

"Don't tell me. The presentation evening."

"How'd you guess?"

"I wish you'd put as much effort into your homework as you have that thing. You'd be top of the class. What is it? Still not decided about the presents?"

"Something like that."

Actually, it wasn't what to buy Hannah and Katie that was on my mind. It wasn't Megan's super-size waterworks, either, show-stopping as those were. It was her listing everyone's qualities that I couldn't get out of my head. What had I got as an accolade? Nothing. Not even best hair bobbles.

This time I knew she hadn't left me out to be spiteful. Whatever our history, Megan was always fair when it came to bigging up her team-mates. So why hadn't she bigged me up? Maybe she'd just forgotten to big me up in the heat of the moment? And when Petra had said Megan would miss *us*, I had a sneaky suspicion "us" hadn't included me.

"Back in a mo'," I said to Mum now.

"All right, sweetie. Don't scuff your varnish now."

"I won't."

☆ ☆ ☆

In my bedroom I booted up my laptop and did something I'd never done before. I typed "Parrs ladies football" into Yahoo. Seconds later there we were on our very own website. I homed in on the Under 11s team shot. How funky did I look in my pink scrunchie and matching pendant? Get in! But me looking stylish wasn't what I was searching for this time.

I worked my way through the photo gallery. Tabinda's dad always took loads of pics during matches. Having said that, the only photo I could find with me in it, other than the team shot, was at the last Hixton Lees match. I was standing on the touchline next to Holly and the caption beneath, written by Katie, read: *Amy asking Hols, "Do shinpads come in pink?" Typical Amy!!!*

I smiled but it wasn't exactly what I was looking for. I tried the match reports next; there was hardly anything about me in there, either. I got a mention in the cup final but I had to scroll back to a year last December for a feeble "Way to go, Minto."

I closed the website down feeling shocked.

I hadn't exactly shone at the game, had I? No wonder Megan hadn't included me in her hall of fame.

I told myself I didn't care. Football had never been my thing and I'd never pretended it had. So what if Megan and the others didn't rate me? Hannah had always said it's the taking part that matters and I'd taken part whatever those reports or photos showed.

But as I returned to the living room I realized I did care. I wanted to be remembered as more than Gemma's ditzy friend. I wanted what everyone else had. A football legacy. I wanted to be a proper Parr.

And that was the biggest shock of all.

7

"How Can We Help?"

An Amy Minter Friendship Dilemma

It turned out I wasn't the only one who'd spent the evening agonizing over Megan's outburst. It was the first thing Gemma brought up at after-school club the next day. "You know, it never occurred to me that they'll miss us as much as they'll miss Hannah and Katie."

"Well, they're bound to; we're legends," Eve pointed out.

"Why don't we do something special just for them at the presentation evening? We could sing a song maybe? I don't mean just the four of us – I mean

Lucy and Nika too. All the leavers," Holly said.

I gasped out loud. Give that girl a gold star and matching earrings! What an opportunity! Not singing – forget dumb old singing. Let's get back to basics. "Or we could have an actual match. Six inside. Leavers versus Stayers," I said, all excited.

"You mean six *a* side?" Gemma asked.

"Whatever." I could see it now. I'd score a hat-trick, then drop back in defence and be brave there, and head for the middle and do a few tackle things. "Amy, that was outstanding," Megan would gush. Meanwhile, Mum could video the whole thing for posterity. Sorted.

But Eve had other ideas. "Nah. Too complicated. We'd have to bring a change of clothes and everything. A song's best. I'll talk to Lucy and Nika at school tomorrow. Where will we rehearse, though? They won't be able to come here. They do other stuff straight from school. We could meet up at my house on Saturdays? Nika only lives a couple of streets away and you lot can get lifts. Right?"

I was going to ask Eve who'd died and made her Committee Queen but Gemma and Holly immediately agreed with her! So rude! I was well miffed they hadn't even considered my match idea. When I broached it later with Gemma she just laughed and said she thought I'd been kidding. That was just what I needed – another sign of how beneath their radar my opinions were when it came to football.

8

RELATIONSHIPS:
When MUMS Fall IN Lurve
– the Telltale Signs

Mum was late picking me up. That meant I
was last to leave and Mrs Rose was not a happy
bunny. Nor was I. The presentation evening was
turning into one big stress-fest. Singing wasn't what
I'd signed up for. Using up my Saturdays wasn't
what I'd signed up for. Feeling like a freak wasn't
what I'd signed up for. "Would it kill you to be on
time for once?" I sighed as Mum led the way back to
the car.

"Sorry, honeybun. Got caught up in things."

"The tanning booth, by any chance?"

She was very orange.

"I needed a top-up. Shane's coming for supper tomorrow and I don't want him to see me all pasty-looking now, do I?"

"Tomorrow? Midweek? Why?"

"Why not?"

"Because I'm not in the mood."

"Tough."

"Tough to you, too."

"Where are you going?" Mum asked as I opened the back car door instead of the front.

"Well, I don't want spray stuff rubbing off on me, do I?" Unfortunately the back seat still had the boxes of T-shirts hogging it. I groaned. "Haven't you got rid of these yet?"

"What's it look like?"

"It looks like I'm going to be sitting with Mrs Tantastic."

She laughed as I slammed the back door shut and slid in beside her. We drove in silence for a minute and then she said, "By the way, I meant to ask you what you thought of Shane? You know – the other night."

I shrugged. "He wasn't awful, apart from calling you Debs."

"That's it? That's the only fault you could find?"

"Give me a chance. I only saw him for two minutes."

"I'm going to. Why do you think he's coming to supper tomorrow?"

Hmm. This had "set up" written all over it. I glanced at her. To my amazement, colour was spreading all along her cheeks and up the whole of her neck. At first I thought it was the Fake Bake still fake-baking but then I realized she was proper blushing. "Mum?"

"Uh-huh."

"You're really keen on him, aren't you?"

"I think I am, babe."

"And is he really keen on you?"

The blush deepened. We're talking cherry wood here. "I think he is."

She turned and smiled, her eyes all faraway and shiny. The last time I'd seen her look like that was in the January sales when she found a Gucci handbag with seventy per cent off. Wow! My mum had fallen in love and I'd missed it. This was major.

At home there was a round-robin email from Hannah telling us the presentation evening had been brought forward to 4 p.m. from 7 p.m. *We thought we should have the U11s separate from the Seniors, so we could spend more time with you all*, she wrote.

Normally, I'd have written a chatty reply but the thing with Shane and my mum had thrown me, so I just sent her a quick, *OK!*

I spent the next day focusing on Shane's visit. When Mum was in the gooey stages of a relationship she tended to get a bit carried away. I knew from experience suppers led to sleepovers and sleepovers led to moving in. There had been two moving-ins in my lifetime and both were disastrous. First came Jim with the bitter ex-wife who kept turning up at the shop and calling Mum awful names. Then there was Rick with the three kids. He was all right but the kids were a total nightmare, especially when they stayed at weekends and during holidays. They wrecked my wardrobe. It took me weeks to get my separates colour coordinated again.

So you can't blame me for being a little wary of Shane. I knew he didn't have an ex-wife or any kids but there had to be something bogus in his background, and if there was, I needed to know about it.

When Wednesday evening came I grilled that guy good and proper. This is what I found out:

- ☆ He is 37 and a Capricorn.
- ☆ He runs a printing firm called Monaghan's with two branches in Mowborough – one on Penrith Street and one on the industrial estate.
- ☆ His last name is Monaghan (see above!).

☆ As well as his sister Kay, who's an administration assistant, he's got another sister called Rachael, who makes silver jewellery.

☆ He's seen Coldplay fifteen times.

☆ He takes one sugar in his tea and none in coffee.

☆ He doesn't always wear capri pants (phew).

He seemed to want to find out as much about me as I did about him. For every question I asked he returned serve. "So your mum was telling me you play football, Amy?"

"Sort of."

"You should come with me and Ash to the NEC on Saturday. There's a massive event on called Grassroots. We went last year. It's great."

I didn't even hesitate. "OK."

What better way to get to know the guy than to spend a whole day with him?

☆ ☆ ☆

Of course the committee were devastated when I told them I couldn't make the first rehearsal. When I say devastated, I mean hacked off. "But it's all arranged," Eve complained.

"Sorry. It's just not ... convenient," I said and left it at that. I am as open as anything about most subjects but when it comes to Mum's boyfriends I like to keep things private. After what happened with Jim and Rick you can hardly blame me.

9

Getting to Know You

An Amy Minter Special Feature

My first dilemma that Saturday was what to wear. After about forty changes I decided on the Parrs away shirt. I never, ever wear sportswear if I'm not actually playing a sport – it's so not the look for me – but I decided to make an exception. Go me and my ability to dress appropriately for the occasion. "Aw. Sporty Spice," Mum said when I went downstairs to the shop to wait.

Shane arrived just as Mum was opening up. I was tidying the Powdered Egg range – that's this retro 1950s stuff little kids look adorable in – but I kept sneaking glances at them while they chatted across the counter. Although their conversation was well boring it was obvious they were dying for a smooch. "I'll go and wait in the car, shall I?"

"It's the black Laguna," Shane called after me. "Tell Ash I'll be one minute."

There wasn't anyone in a black Laguna but there was a boy with scraggy hair in jeans and a burgundy-and-navy-striped football shirt kicking a ball against the wall near by. I presumed this was The Neph.

I cleared my throat, planning to introduce myself, but before I had a chance the boy did something weird. As the ball rebounded off the wall, instead of kicking it again he caught it on his laces. For a while he balanced it there, perfectly still, his arms outstretched and then – don't ask me how because I'm sure I never blinked – the ball was cradled in the curve of his neck. He did that about three times.

"That's so clever," I told him. He stopped, turned and scowled at me. "I'm Amy," I said quickly. "I'm coming with you today?"

He managed a shrug.

O-kaaay, I thought, not entirely surprised by the lukewarm reception. I mean, I was gate-crashing his buddy time with his uncle. I tried again. "I like your team colours. Do you play locally?"

"What? You think I play for Barcelona?" he scoffed and gave me the kind of look Karren Brady gives the contestants on *The Apprentice* when they've said something really, really stupid. He turned his back on me and started pounding the ball against the wall again.

How rude! As I sent a thousand mental daggers into the back of his shirt, I peered at the name written on it: Messi. Huh! What a perfect nickname given his hair.

"Right, then!" Shane said, careering round the corner, a huge grin on his face. "Party time!"

The journey was tortuous. I sat in the back and it was football, football, football all the way. Shane did his best to involve me but I wished he hadn't.

It soon became obvious I didn't know anything about the sport and he had to lower the bar until finally we arrived at stuff I could answer. "What's your team called, Amy?" Yes, that low.

"The Parrs."

"What league are they in?"

"Nettie Honeyball."

Ashley snorted. "That is such a made-up name."

"Excuse me, she was totally real," I told him, quoting bits I remembered from the website about her organizing one of the first women's matches.

Shane whistled. "Eighteen ninety-five? That long ago? Well, I never knew that. And who are your favourite female players today?"

Busted! Again! I so wanted to reel off a list of names but I didn't know any. "Gemma Hurst and ... um ... Lucy Skidmore."

"Sure it's not Betty Offside?" Ashley asked.

"Oh, now I remember where I've seen you before. Weren't you on the Comedy Store last week?" I said.

That shut him up for about two minutes but I was

so out of my depth I needed a lifeboat. When they started talking about the last Women's World Cup and how excellent it had been I pretended I was texting. Unfortunately I couldn't text real people. All the real people were in a singing rehearsal I was now *so* wishing I'd attended.

We arrived at the NEC about half-past eleven. The place was heaving and we were in the ticket queue for ages. "Quick, Uncle Shane. He starts in two minutes," Ashley said, jabbing the programme we'd picked up at the entrance.

"Who does?" I asked.

Ashley turned to me, a smile on his face for once. "Billy Wingrove."

"Who does he play for?" I asked, expecting him to roll his eyes and say, "Don't you even know that?" But he was quite civilized.

"No one. He's a freestyler."

"A what?"

"You'll see."

Tickets bought, we followed the herd into the main arena. There were loads of stands all down the sides displaying all sorts of things from new kits to football nets to power drinks. I perked up. It was like a shopping mall for football fans. Bliss! Maybe I could find Hannah and Katie's presents here?

But Ashley made it clear he wasn't here for the stands. He led us through to where the crowd was thickest until we pitched up at the front of a roped-off area. Inside it were two men in thin long-sleeved jerseys and football shorts, hands behind their backs, legs slightly apart, each with a ball on the ground next to him, waiting to start. "Oh, Jeremy Lynch is with Billy today," Ashley gasped. I'm guessing that was meant to mean something.

Before I had time to ask which was Billy and which was Jeremy, music started blasting out of the speakers near by and the men began performing. In perfect synchronicity they jumped, juggled, flipped, twisted and turned with their ball so fast my head hurt. Sometimes they did exactly the same trick side by side – like maybe rolling the ball from their foot to their knee and then spinning their bodies round so they were bouncing the ball from their heel to their calf. A second later they'd be sitting back to back, their quick feet passing the two balls quickly back and forth over their heads so they crossed mid-air without colliding. These men were like acrobats or seals or acrobatic seals even. Whatever they were, their skills were impressive.

I glanced across at Ashley. He wasn't smiling and nodding in admiration like everyone else. He was just staring. Staring and concentrating so hard. He's trying to memorize it, I realized. When the exhibition ended and everyone clapped he just stood there.

"Billy and Jeremy will be signing copies of their new DVD in one minute," someone announced.

"Are you going to buy it?" I asked Ashley.

"I've already got it," he said. His adoring eyes followed the men as they made their way to the dump bin where all the DVDs were stacked.

"He practises every day. It drives Kay potty."
Shane laughed.

Ashley turned to Shane, his eyes shining. "You've
got to practise. How else are you going to get any
good at it? Freestyling takes just as much skill as
playing football. More, probably. A lot of footballers
can't do what Billy does."

When I heard that my whole body tingled. "Really?"

"Really. I mean a few can. Ronaldo and Naymar
are ace, but it's more an exhibition thing really. For
doing in front of a crowd at a big match and stuff."

"Do ... can girls freestyle?" I asked because I had
this idea growing in my head.

"Yeah. Of course. Laura Biondo's good and so's
Robyn Clancy."

I grinned. That was all I needed to know. "Ashley,"
I said, "will you lend me your Billy Wingrove DVD?"

That night I watched the DVD all the way through,
becoming more and more excited as the idea I'd
had at the NEC grew and grew. I was going to end

my days as a Parr on a high after all. I was going to *freestyle* my way into Megan's hall of fame. Not just Megan's but everyone's, including the mighty grump herself, Jenny-Jane Bayliss.

"Did you have a nice day?" Mum asked as she came in to kiss me goodnight.

"I had a brilliant day," I told her.

10

Project Ambition

Amy Minter Shows U How 2 AIM HIGH

Next morning I leapt out of bed raring to go. Ashley told me it had taken him months to perfect the trick he'd done in the car park (called a neck catch B.T.W.). I had two weeks. No time to lose.

That was when I realized the flaw in my plan. I didn't have a football. I mean, why would I? I sighed and watched the Billy Wingrove DVD again, miming some of the moves with an invisible ball instead. I must have looked hilarious.

During breakfast Mum asked how I wanted to

spend Sunday. "Aren't you seeing Shane?" I asked.

"No," she said then hesitated. "Amy?"

"Mum."

"You know the other day when I said I was keen on him?"

I reached across for seconds of granola. I needed extra fuel if I was going to be laying down some freestyling moves. "Uh-huh."

"Don't get carried away, will you? I don't want you choosing bridesmaids' dresses or anything."

"Oh, I know that."

"You do?"

"For sure, babe. He hasn't seen you without make-up yet."

"True." She laughed and began sifting through yesterday's post. "Bills, bills, postcard, bills, bills, bills."

"Who's the postcard from?"

Mum flipped it over. "Chico and Luisa."

"Who?"

"Carlos and Rosa's grandchildren. The postman's messed up again."

"I'll take it!" I said, grabbing the postcard as I remembered something.

Five minutes later, I was in my bedroom with Chico and Luisa's yellow-and-black plastic football, borrowed from the toy box Carlos kept for them for when they visited. I decided to concentrate on perfecting my keepy-uppies first so I rolled up my bedside rug to give myself max floorboard space.

Keepy-uppies are pips. Anyone can do them, right? I've watched Eve and Gemma do them before matches and there's nothing to it. All you have to do is bounce the ball about on your foot or your knee or your head and keep it off the ground. Only in my case, keeping it off the ground meant sending it from my foot to my knee to my dressing table or my lampshade or my window. One attempt clattered into the mantlepiece and knocked my favourite photo frame on to the marble hearth. Luckily the glass didn't break but I had to spend the next five minutes clearing away all my breakables and reassuring Mum

I wasn't trashing the place. "I'm fine. I'm fine," I told her when she stuck her head round the door to see what all the noise was.

I didn't get the hang of keepy-uppies at all and went to bed feeling disheartened. If I couldn't even do the basics I had no chance of putting on a performance for the Parrs in less than two weeks' time. What had I been thinking? Amy Minter, freestyler? Free-faller more like.

But as I tried to get to sleep that night I kept seeing Jenny-Jane pirouetting around the function room and remembering Megan missing me out of her hall of fame speech. A determination burned in me. I would do this. I would master keepy-uppies if it killed me. I sat up and reached for my alarm, setting it for an hour earlier than normal.

Over the next couple of days I tried sooooo hard, but by Wednesday I still couldn't manage more than two knee bounces in a row no matter how often

I watched Billy "show-off" Wingrove's stooopid DVD. In desperation, I called round at Miro's to ask Carlos for help but he laughed and said his football-playing days were over. Shane was busy in the evenings helping his sister Rachael design a special booklet for her new range of jewellery so he was no use either.

Of course, the obvious people to teach me were under my nose at after-school club but that was a no-no. This had to be a surprise for them as much as for Megan and co. Besides, at after-school club I was too occupied playing catch-up with the song. Apparently, it wasn't enough to just sing it. We had to change all the lyrics to make them personal to the Parrs and dance as well. My team-mates never can do things by halves.

Soooooooooo that only left one person I could think of: Ashley.

I plucked up the courage to call him on Thursday. At first I pretended I just wanted to chat about his hero Billy Wingrove but then I came clean and told him how I had been rubbish at football and wanted to make amends. "So this would be like my last chance to impress them," I told him.

I waited, cringing inside, expecting him to tell me to bog off. But he didn't. "Sure. Why not?"

"Sunday?" I suggested quickly before he changed his mind.

"Can't. Can do Saturday morning."

I chewed my lip. On Saturday morning I was meant to be at Eve's. I couldn't miss two rehearsals in a row, could I? But my keepy-uppies were pathetic. They had to take priority. I'd just have to promise to put in tons of overtime on the song midweek. They'd understand. They were my buddies, right? "OK. See you Saturday morning then, Messi. Thanks."

"Messy?"

"That is your nickname, isn't it?"

He snorted down the phone and hung up. What was that about? Boys!

☆ ☆ ☆

You know I said the committee would understand about me missing Saturday's rehearsal? I was wrong.

Eve glowered at me. "Amy, how exactly are we meant to practise the song without you? The dance routine was totally out of balance last week. We had to put a cushion where you were meant to be."

"Was it a stylish cushion?"

"Amy!"

Ah. Not a good time for a wisecrack, then. I had to think of something convincing quickly. "Hello? Buying Hannah and Katie's present. When else am I supposed to do it?"

"Maybe straight afterwards? I could come with you then," Gemma offered.

Holly smiled. "I could too."

"Me three," Eve added.

Well, that excuse worked. I pretended to be outraged. "Are you kidding me? I can't get presents of that magnitude in half a day!"

"Well, whatever you get had better be spectacular then, that's all I can say," Eve said.

11

"The Only Real Failure in Life is the Failure to Try"

– found on Amy Minter's Calendar of Inspirational Quotes

Ashley arrived promptly at the shop on Saturday morning at ten o'clock. "Come upstairs," I told him – he was looking seriously out of place among the babygros. Mum gave us a silly little wave as we left. I hadn't told her why I'd invited Ashley round. I just said we were hanging out. By that she thought I meant I had a crush on him and had been humming "Amy and Ashley sitting in a tree, k-i-s-s-i-n-g" since Thursday night. Parents can be so immature sometimes.

The first thing Ashley did when we got to my room was to laugh his head off at my ball. "What's that?"

"A cabbage. What's it look like?"

He shook his head and slipped off his backpack. "Good job I've brought mine." It turned out Carlos's ball was way too light and that was why it had been hard to control. Ashley's football was more like the ones we used in matches. "Right," he said, dropping it at my feet and standing back. "Show me what you've got."

Not a lot, was the answer, even with the right equipment.

"We need to go outside," he decided after I'd almost blasted the TV off its wall bracket.

"OK. I'll find a rug."

"A rug?"

"Well, I'm not lying on the dirty car-park floor."

"Why do you need to lie down?"

"For when I'm doing my routine. I'm well up for

one of those things Billy does when he rolls the ball along his whole body."

"Even I can't do that."

"Maybe I'm more supple than you. I used to do ballet, you know."

"When is this for again?"

"Next week."

"No chance."

I felt the blood drain from my face. "I have to."

"Forget the rug," Ashley said.

In the car park he made me work on my keepy-uppies for almost TWO hours. He wanted me to repeat them and repeat them so that I broke my personal best every time. "I'm sooo bored," I told him when I'd finally reached five in a row. "And I ache all over."

"Fine. Let's pack it in, then."

I groaned. "No. I can't."

"Look, once you've cracked this you'll be laughing. Keepy-uppies are all about control.

Brazilian players do them all the time as part of their game. Here, check this out."

Glad of the breather, I watched a YouTube clip on his iPhone of two players heading the ball to one another a few times before they switched to these whizzy leg things. They're hard to describe because the players were doing them so fast. Basically you start by balancing the ball on your foot, then flip it into the air. Then, while it's in the air, you orbit your leg around it and catch it again on your foot. To do that once would be impressive; to do it loads and loads in a row – impress–*ive*!

"I like those," I said.

"That's called 'Around the World'." He tucked away his mobile and demonstrated. "You just kick the ball lightly in the air then revolve your whole leg round it clockwise or anticlockwise in a complete orbit before it falls."

"You make it look so easy."

"I do, don't I?" He grinned and then checked his watch. "I've got to go."

"Must you?"

"Yep. Meeting my mates."

"Can't you come tomorrow?"

"Nope. Dad's taking me out."

"Will you come if he bails on you again?"

As soon as I said it I knew I'd boobed. Ashley's face turned – well – ashen. "He won't bail."

"I'm sorry. I didn't mean..."

He stuffed his ball back in his bag. I felt awful. "Ash, I'm really sorry. I say such totally stupid things sometimes. I do it all the time. I get it from my mum..."

"Not your daddy, then?" he sneered.

I felt my stomach clench. "The only thing I get from that loser is my school fees and that's only because Mum took him to court."

Now Ashley seemed more curious than annoyed. "Wow! That must have been some divorce."

I stared at the ground. "Hardly. They'd have to have been married to get divorced and as he was already married to someone else that would have been tricky..."

"Nice guy."

I broke off. I hadn't even mentioned the two other kids he had. His *real* daughters (who were totally minging if their pictures on Facebook were anything to go by). My throat felt tight. I looked up and tried to smile. "I can't believe I told you that! Nobody else knows any of that. Not even my best friend."

"I won't say anything."

"Good. 'Cos if you do I'd have to kill you."

"You can't kill me. If you kill me you'll never learn how to freestyle."

"Dur! Obviously I'll kill you *after* you've taught me."

He laughed and checked his watch again. "I suppose another hour wouldn't hurt."

"Yay!"

I tried. I really tried but five keepy-uppies in a row was my max, despite doing what Ashley had instructed and keeping my eye on the ball all the time and concentrating hard. I was so disappointed I was almost in tears. Five keepy-uppies would be over in five seconds. Some performance that would be.

"This means a lot to you, doesn't it?" he said.

I nodded, too scared to speak in case I started blubbing.

"Look, what if I came too? You know, helped you out a bit on the night? I could do all the hard moves and you could do the keepy-uppies and maybe even a couple of Around the Worlds in between?"

I was *soooooooooo* tempted but I shook my head. It would only complicate things. "Thanks, but I don't think that would work."

"In that case you'd better hang on to this, Nettie." He handed me his football. Sweet!

All that evening and the whole of Sunday I practised and practised. I attempted Around the World a few times but I could not get the hang of it. The hardest part wasn't getting my leg to orbit the ball, it was stopping the ball bouncing away after my leg had finished the orbiting. I was uber gutted. I would have loved at least one of those in my act. It was such a neat trick. I sighed. I needed more time.

12

Is Lying to Your Friends Ever Acceptable?

An Amy Minter True Life Dilemma

"What do you mean you can't go to after-school club after today?" Mum asked.

"I just can't. Not this week. I need to come home straight from school."

"So you're telling me I have to close the shop early to pick you up?"

"I can always walk."

That was never going to happen. Mum thinks there's a weirdo on every corner. I'm not even allowed to go to the botanical gardens without four

Alsatians and an armed guard. She tutted and said she'd "sort something out".

I'd put Mum in a fix but that was nothing compared to how the committee reacted. "So basically you're not taking part in the song. Is that what you're saying?" Eve fumed when I told them that I wouldn't be at after-school club for the rest of the week.

"No! I know all the words. And you've shown me the steps. It's not rocket science, is it?"

Eve's eyes almost shot out of her head. "Not what? Oh, you take the biscuit, you do, Minter." She turned on her heel and stormed towards the baking table, which was kind of appropriate when you think about it.

"Why aren't you coming, really?" Holly asked.

I shrugged. I couldn't think of a good enough reason so I thought of a flippant one instead. "What can I say? The new series of *Project Catwalk* starts tomorrow. You know me. I can't possibly miss that."

You want to know the worst thing? Even though

that was the lamest excuse ever, she didn't bat an eyelid. She really thought I'd put a TV fashion show before the Parrs. "Oh, right," she said.

Gemma just sat there, a deep, deep frown on her face.

Gemma waited until school the next day to collar me. "You've totally lost interest in the presentation evening, haven't you?"

I shuffled in my seat. "No. It's not that..."

"I guessed you would. You haven't been the same since all the plans for the Jump-leads and things fell through. Now there's not much organizing to do, you're bored. It figures. You've never liked football. I guess I should be grateful you held on this long," Gemma said.

What? And *what* again? Right, I thought, this has gone far enough. I'd have to tell her the truth. "Gemma..."

Before I had chance to explain she pulled me towards her and gave me this massive hug. "Don't worry. After Saturday, it will all be over and you can forget I ever forced you to wear a pair of smelly shinpads or made you get your hair wet in the rain or..."

"But, Gemma..." I tried to pull away but she just hugged me harder.

"Thank you for being there when I really needed you. I'd never have gone back for that last match if it wasn't for you and I'd definitely not be going for trials at the centre of excellence."

"You're going for trials at the centre of excellence?" I gasped.

She finally let go of me and blushed. "I didn't want to say anything in case it didn't happen, but I had a letter this morning inviting me to attend."

"Wow! That's amazing!"

"Don't tell anyone. I'll only get wound up if people make a fuss. I'm nervous enough already and they're not until June."

I clapped my hand on her back. "Don't worry, girlfriend. I'll get you through this."

She smiled. "I know you will. You get me through everything. That's why I need you to promise you'll come to the final dress rehearsal at Eve's on Saturday morning? Please? And you'll do the song at the presentation evening? No matter how lame you think it is?"

"Of course I'll be there. Just try and stop me."

"Thank you," she sniffed and was back on the hugging thing.

13

When Disaster Strikes

An Amy Minter True Life Story

I now had another reason to get my freestyle routine perfect. I wanted Gemma to feel as proud of me as I was of her. I made use of the extra time and practised soooo hard all week. By Friday my legs ached like mad and my floorboards needed revarnishing but it was worth it. I didn't have a long routine, but I knew I had enough to show that I wasn't a total waste of space with a football.

I grabbed Gemma's arm as we headed for lunch on Friday. "I can't wait for tomorrow. What time are we meeting at Eve's?"

"Ten-ish."

"Cool. I'll be there."

"You'd better be. We can show you the changes."

"Changes?"

"To the song. We twiddled with the end a bit yesterday to make it more upbeat. Don't worry; it isn't difficult. In fact, it's right up your street."

"Intriguing. And are we still having lunch in town together afterwards?"

"Yep."

"And your dad is still OK to drop me off at home?"

"Yep."

"Great. Holly's picking me up at three for the presentation evening, so I'll see you at the club at about quarter to four," I said as we joined the lunch queue. I squinted at the menu. "OK. Chicken casserole or lasagne and don't say lasagne. I'm sure they used polystyrene instead of pasta last time."

Gemma laughed and collected the cutlery and beakers. "Oh, by the way, you know when you bring the presents?"

"The presents?"

"Yeah, dummy, the presents for Hannah and Katie. We drew lots and Dylan and Nika are going to hand them over, so if you sneak them into the back of the bar as soon as you arrive, they'll collect them from there. Are they heavy? Will you need help?"

"Um..."

"What did you get, anyway? You haven't even told me yet. I bet it's something brilliant."

When I didn't answer she peered at me. "Are you OK? You look pale?"

Pale? Is that all? My heart had stopped and all I looked was pale? The presents! I hadn't bought the presents! How I managed to keep myself together until Mum picked me up at the end of the day I don't know but once she did I totally broke down. That scene in the gazebo with Megan? Nothing. Not even close to what I was doing now. "Don't cry, baby, don't cry. We'll think of something," Mum promised as she drove through town.

"The p ... presents. I can't be-be-lieve I didn't buy

the presents!" I howled.

"What if I pull in here?" Mum asked as we passed the main shopping arcade.

"Noooooooooooo. Those shops are totally naff."

"How about the Butter Market? There's a lovely florist's..."

"Nooooo! It's got to be something special..."

"Where, then?"

"We'll ha-ha-have t-to go to B-Buh-Birmingham."

"Birmingham is two hours away. The shops will be shut by the time we get there."

"Not if you drive really fast."

Mum got irritated then and told me to stop being silly. I got irritated back and told her I wasn't. The thing was, if we didn't get them tonight, when would we? I had a rehearsal all morning and I daren't back out of that. The only other opportunity I'd have was about an hour at lunchtime and I would be with Gemma then. I could just see her face when I told her what I was doing. After all the fuss I'd made about choosing the perfect gift she'd never forgive

me even if I did a *hundred* keepy-uppies later on.
I pleaded with Mum again. "Wh ... what about
Leicester? Leicester's only an hour."

Mum ignored me and turned down Penrith Street.
"Why are we going down here?" I wailed. "There
aren't any gift shops down here!"

"Because I said I'd call in at Shane's."

That made me bawl even harder. Here I was in
the middle of a crisis and she was calling in at her
boyfriend's. "Mum! What part of I HAVE to buy
presents don't you understand?"

She ignored me (her *only* child B.T.W.) and drew
up outside a row of dull-looking shops, yanked on
the handbrake, checked her lipstick in the mirror and
then passed me another tissue. "Wipe your eyes,
babe. Shane'll think we've had a bereavement."

I snatched the tissue from her hand. "I don't care
what he thinks. I need to go shopping!"

"What you need is to be more organized."

That made me so mad; I got out of the passenger
door and slammed it so hard one of the boxes of

T-shirts on the back seat slid into my headrest. "Me? You're the one who's not organized or these things wouldn't still be here, would they?"

"F.Y.I. I am organized, honey. I gave the courier until today to collect. He's missed his deadline, so these are going to Oxfam first thing tomorrow."

"You might as well take me with them."

"La-la-la..." Mum sang as I followed her into the printer's.

"This is such a waste of time," I sobbed, my chest heaving painfully in and out. "You don't love me at all."

Half an hour later we came back outside. "Feeling better now, Ames?" Mum asked.

I nodded. "Yes, Mum."

"Not cross now?"

"Not cross." How could I be cross when Shane had come up with the perfect solution to my present problem? I won't tell you any more now. All I will tell you is the man is a genius.

14

And Now the End Is Near...

The day of the presentation finally arrived.

I woke up feeling soooo nervous and soooo excited.
I checked my final "to do" list. It wasn't how I
imagined it would look but here it is:

1) Practise freestyle routine

2) Last rehearsal at Eve's

3) Lunch with Gem/collect presents/get ready

4) Get lift in with Hols

5) Sneak presents into bar

6) Hide A.'s ball somewhere accessible in
   function room 4 my bit

7) Do my amazing routine

8) Collapse from exhaustion

The first thing on my list was pips. My keepy-uppies were so well practised I could do them in my sleep. I left Ashley's ball and my trainers on my bed, made a few phone calls and headed for Eve's.

The rehearsal was tickety-boo too. Eve said something like, "Nice of you to show up," when I arrived but I'd been expecting that so I just smiled serenely and gave her the massive box of chocolates I'd brought with me.

"Bribery won't work," she huffed before tearing off the cellophane and taking a deep sniff of the top layer. Her eyebrows rose higher and higher. "OK, I lied!" she declared and swooped. Those caramels never stood a chance.

The rehearsal was good fun. I'd forgotten how sweet Nika is and how witty Lucy can be and I wished I'd been at all of them. Still, I couldn't be in two places at once and if sacrificing a couple of mornings with my team-mates was what it took to prove to them I wasn't the football-lightweight they thought I was, then so be it.

And I did still have it to prove. The song we were singing, "So Long, Farewell" from *The Sound of Music* had quite a sad ending.

"Aren't we changing the ending?" I asked. "Gemma said you wanted something more upbeat?"

Lucy nodded. "We did. And that's where you come in."

"Me?"

"We thought it would be funnier if, as we all trooped off, you stepped forward and said something like: 'Oh, and don't forget, the one thing a footballer needs is...' Then you wait a second and go: 'A really good moisturizer...'"

I scowled. "And why would I say something as shallow as that?"

Everyone cracked up. Gemma included. "Amy. It's one of your quotes. We wanted something typically 'you' to finish off with. To make them smile."

I sniffed. What I had planned wouldn't make them smile. It would blow them away.

Next was lunch in town with Gemma and her dad, Kriss. "Can we go by Penrith Street first?" I asked Kriss. "I need to pick up the presents."

"A printer's?" Gemma noted as she followed me in.

"Yep. For all your printing needs. Business cards, invitations, letterheads, mugs, coasters..." I said, pointing to the different samples on display.

"OK."

"And T-shirts, I hope," I added, beaming at Carol, Shane's assistant.

She recognized me from yesterday and grinned. "I'll just get Shane for you," she said.

"Shane?" Gemma asked.

"Oh, just one of my many business contacts."

Two minutes later Shane arrived, carrying one large box with two small packages on top. "Here you go, Amy. Hot off the press."

I clapped. "Ohh. This is soooo brilliant."

"Would you like to see them now?"

"Well, of course."

He set the packages aside and took the lid off the box. He pulled out the top XXL T-shirt and handed it over to me. Yes, you guessed it. The T-shirts from Mum's car. Yesterday, between sobs, I'd spotted what Shane's printing shop could do with T-shirts and hey presto! "Yay," I said, holding the T-shirt up against me to show Gemma the team photo across the front. "How cool is this?"

"Neat," Gemma said.

"All you have to do is email a picture and they print it on. There's one for everyone, not just Hannah and Katie. I thought it would be a nice memento. And look..." I turned the T-shirt round so she could see the writing on the back. "Parrs Under 11s, Winners of the Nettie Honeyball Cup, coached by Hannah Preston and Katie Regan, LEGENDS."

Gemma nodded. "It's great," she said, but I could tell from her tone she was thinking, Is that it? Is that what we've spent all the money on?

I turned to Shane and then pointed to the packages. "She had them in, then?"

His eyes twinkled. "She certainly did."

"May we see?"

Shane slid one of the packages towards him. They were wrapped in plain brown paper and tied with a matt silver bow. He undid one of the bows carefully, then pulled out a crushed pink velvet drawstring bag. So sweet! Nestling inside the bag was one of the two identical silver necklaces I'd chosen from his sister Rachael's brochure. The brochure had been lying on the counter last night and I'd flicked through it to try to hide my wet face. There, right on page one, I'd seen the totally perfect gift for our coaches. I could tell from Gemma's reaction that she thought so too. "Oh, it's beautiful. So delicate. I love the tiny footballs," she said.

"Shane's sister made them. She's dead clever."

"I'll pass on your compliments," Shane said, coaxing the necklace back into the bag and muttering that he'd never be able to tie the ribbon back up again with his turnipy thumbs.

While he did that I burrowed into my bag and brought out all the money we'd collected. "Hope that covers it," I said to Carol as pound coins rolled everywhere.

It did but only just. Shane had done the T-shirts for free but of course the necklaces weren't.

"See you later, then. Have a good time," Shane said, holding the door open.

"He was friendly," Gemma said when we were outside.

"Indeed." I smiled.

After that it was crazy busy. We had lunch at Nando's, then Kriss dropped me off at home. I left the presents and T-shirts with Gemma so that she could hand them over when she arrived at the club. It gave me one less thing to stress about.

Upstairs, I packed my trainers and Ashley's ball into a Monsoon bag, had a shower, washed my hair and put on my specially selected outfit. I'd gone deliberately boho to maintain my fashionista rep. Despite the extra prep time I was ready and waiting in the shop for Holly by 2.55 p.m.

Mum was serving a customer, which gave me a chance to go over my plan. So, after we'd finished the song, I'd do the bit about moisturizer (ho ho), then I'd flip my ballet pumps into the audience, pull on the trainers, get out the football and go into my freestyle routine. There'd be stunned silence, followed by cheering (with Megan leading the standing ovation probs). I'd take a bow, maybe sign a few autographs. And cut!

"Angel?" Mum was saying.

"Mmm," I said dreamily, still imagining the shock on JJ's face.

"Holly's here."

So she was, waving frantically at me through the window. Mum gave me a kiss, told me I looked gorgeous and wished me good luck.

I took a deep breath.

This was it.

The presentation evening.

Bring it on!

When we arrived at the function room, it was hectic. Everyone was hyper. Daisy and Dylan were flying round the room pretending to be aeroplanes; Tabinda's dad was rounding everyone up so he could take photos; Eve and Lucy were blowing balloons up and batting them about; and everyone else was crowding around Hannah and Katie.

Good, I thought. All this confusion would give me a chance to hide my bag somewhere. I strode across to the stage area and tucked it behind the curtain. I felt all tingly. In less than an hour I'd be doing my stuff on that parquet flooring. Scary.

The tingling increased when Hannah clapped her hands and gathered us all together. She wasn't in her tracksuit today and looked so different in her sleeveless shift dress and heels. *See, you can look pretty and be sporty*, I wanted to tell JJ.

"It's so fab to see you all," Hannah began, her eyes sweeping round the whole room. She talked about the season and how proud she was of us all and everything we've achieved. Then Mandy drew back the stage curtain to reveal a trestle-table groaning with trophies. I gasped. Not because of the size of the trophies (please – they're not real gold or anything) but because I'd presumed that was where we'd be doing our dance and therefore my routine.

I dug Gemma in the ribs. "Where are we doing the dance?" I whispered.

"On the carpet here," she whispered back.

"Oh," I said, telling myself it didn't matter. I could fetch the ball when I went up for my medal. (F.Y.I. yes, I get a medal. Don't sound so surprised – everybody gets a medal. Last year I stuffed mine in the back of a drawer somewhere and forgot all about it. I wouldn't be doing that this time, though.)

First came the big awards. Lucy won Coaches' Player of the Year and Nika won the Players' Player of the Year. Tabinda and Jenny-Jane shared "Most

Improved" and Megan won "Clubman" for the second year running.

When it was my turn to go up (last – go figure) I was surprised by how emotional I felt. Nobody seemed to be clapping any less heartily for me. In fact, Gemma and Holly were whistling and Daisy shouted, "Go, Amy Mint humbug! We love you!"

I felt my eyes prick with tears as I stared at the gilt disc with a football on it. "Thank you," I whispered as Katie presented it to me.

"You're welcome," she said, then added, "babe," and everyone laughed.

Hannah gave me a huge hug. "I'll miss you."

"Back at you," I replied, my voice breaking. I walked away, sniffing and TOTALLY FORGETTING TO PICK UP MY MONSOON BAG. Nooooooooooooooooooo.

I turned back, intending to fetch it but Hannah was talking again and I didn't want to seem rude, so I just stood there, biting my lip and trying to listen.

"Anyway, thanks for everything and..." She

paused and looked around. "We were hoping to introduce you to the new coach but she's not here yet, so I guess we should all start mingling..."

I felt sick. This was it. The handing over of the presents bit followed by the leavers' song followed by... I swallowed, hoping Hannah and Katie would like the gifts I'd chosen for them. I waited for Nika and Dylan to hand them over, but it was JJ and Tabinda who stepped forward. From behind the stage curtain, Mandy Leggitt unexpectedly produced two huge bouquets of flowers. She handed one bunch to JJ and the other to Tabinda. '"These are for you," JJ said, her voice croaky as she thrust her bouquet at Hannah.

"Aw, these are lovely..." Hannah began. But before she could finish Nika and Dylan had dashed forward with the official prezzies and Lucy was following behind with the box of T-shirts. My stomach did a somersault. The T-shirts were meant for after. Never mind. Never mind.

There was a hush as Hannah and Katie opened

the packages and brought out the velvet bags. I held my breath.

"Aw!" they both said at the same time when they saw the silver necklaces.

Hannah's eyes glistened. "That's fabulous." She held it up for everyone to see. The room filled with "ooh"s and "ahh"s.

"Well done," Gemma said to me, but my mind had already moved forward. It was the song next, surely? And after the song... Argh! My palms were sweaty. "Is this where we do the dance?" I croaked.

"Think so. Eve's going to signal."

I was so nervous and I still hadn't managed to sidle over to the curtains to get the ball. Lucy was blocking my way. She was waiting for the fuss over the flowers and gifts to die down before she presented the T-shirts to Hannah and Katie. "I'd give them now," I suggested, wanting her to move out of the way so I could sneak across to the stage – but just as she stepped forward Mr Shah appeared out of nowhere. What was he doing getting in on the act? Oh, crumbs. He was going to make a speech!

He went on for AGES about Hannah and Katie's contributions, wishing "the ladies" luck in the future, blah-blah-blah. It was all fair enough and I totally agreed with every word but COME ON!

Lucy was straight in with the T-shirts the second he finished. "Amy had these done specially for us all..."

Everybody looked at me and I blushed my head off. "Just a small … um ... thank you," I said as the T-shirts were given out. I could have – should have – fetched my bag then, but I was torn between doing that and watching everyone's faces as they read the writing on the T-shirts and tried them on. In the end, I went for watching – and laughing. Daisy and Dylan's came to their ankles.

Then Gemma grabbed my hand and I really started to sweat. It was time for the singing, and after the singing...

Eve called for everyone's attention. "Wait up, dudes. There's more. You didn't think the leavers would just walk off into the sunset, did you? No chance. We've got a song we'd like to sing for Hannah, Katie and all the rest of you – Meggo, Petra, Tabs, JJ, Psycho One and Psycho Two. The best team-mates anyone could have. This is for you…"

Everyone shuffled back to make space for us as we lined up. Holly, Nika and Eve on my left, Gemma and Lucy on my right.

The bag! I still hadn't got the bag! Too late. The music had started and we were off. I had words to sing. And I did sing them, loud and clear along with everyone else but it was really difficult. My mind kept jumping to the next bit – my bit. Then, just as I was about to deliver my line about moisturizer, Daisy leapt up and yelled, "Sing it again!"

That wasn't meant to happen. I should have known it would but it wasn't meant to.

So we had to sing it again, only this time everybody joined in. "So long, farewell, *auf wiedersehen,* gooodbyeeeeeeeeeeee."

As we neared the end for a second time I could see Daisy and Dylan both getting ready to leap up and ask for another encore. I couldn't bear it. I had to freestyle now or I'd burst. I stepped forward and garbled, "All you need is a really good moisturizer and I've got some in my bag," or something stupid like that. Then I darted across to the curtain thinking I wouldn't even bother with my trainers. I'd just freestyle in my pumps.

But it wasn't there. My bag with everything in it wasn't there! I couldn't breathe. "I left a bag ... a Monsoon one..."

Mandy, who was near by, smiled. "Oh, sorry, duck. I didn't know what it was. I moved it downstairs when I was hiding the flowers. It's safe behind the bar..."

What? You crazy woman! Why would you even do that?

I took the stairs two at a time, grabbed the bag and dashed back upstairs, but by the time I'd come back the entire scene had shifted. People had splintered into groups. Gemma had been hijacked by Hannah and Katie, Holly was at the buffet with Lucy. The tune from *The Sound of Music* had been replaced by something by the Black Eyed Peas. Everyone was chatting and smiling and mingling.

Eve and Nika were nearest the door. Eve thumped me on my back. "Brilliant way to end, dude. The bag thing. Nice touch."

"But..."

"The song went really well. Everyone loved it," Nika added.

Eve flung her arms round us both. "Right, teamies. Time to par-tay."

That's when I realized there was absolutely no point in trying to get my freestyle act in now. The moment had gone. So totally and so utterly GONE. "Um ... back in a min," I said. I turned and went back downstairs.

In the car park, I up-ended the bag and watched the ball roll across the uneven tarmac and come to rest in the gully at the edge of the pitch. I sighed, knowing I'd never play on that grass again. I was surprised at how that tugged at me.

I bounced the ball a couple of times on my knee and then automatically dropped into my routine. Five keepy-uppies followed by an Around the World. Five keepy-uppies followed by an Around the World. Again and again.

Once I'd started I couldn't stop. It was instinctive now, like swallowing or cringing at my teacher's hideous taste in cardigans. At some point I became aware that I'd beaten my PB. I had got seven, then eight keepy-uppies in a row. My heart began beating faster. Eight! Wait until I told Ashley.

I kept going. My headband started falling in front of my eyes but I ignored it. I'd do blind keepy-uppies. Even Billy Wingrove couldn't do that, bet you. I felt my feet getting faster, my arms tilting and swaying as I fought to keep my balance. Six-seven-eight. Eight again! I laughed out loud. Go me!

"Wow! Well done, you."

I stopped, startled by the unexpected interruption. I looked up to see a woman staring at me. "Hello," she said. "I'm Sian Lewis. I'm taking over from

Hannah and Katie. I was meant to come earlier, but I got stuck on that daft bypass."

"Oh."

"I can tell you're a Parr."

"Pardon?"

"I can tell you're a Parr. Hannah said you were all as keen as mustard but I hadn't realized how keen. Keepy-uppies on a party night? That's dedication."

"If you think I'm keen you should see the rest of them," I told her.

She smiled. "I'm looking forward to it."

"Seriously, though? You can tell I'm a Parr?" I asked, falling into step beside her as we headed inside to the party.

"Definitely."

A slow smile spread across my face. "That is so cool," I said.

Final Whistle

You know what? When Sian said,
"I can tell you're a Parr", my
disappointment at not getting the
chance to freestyle in front of
everyone evaporated in an instant.
That was my accolade right there.
What more could I ask for?

I knew something else too. As I
walked back into that function room
with the new coach, I realized I was
going to carry on playing sport. No
way was I going to let all that hard
work and those hours of practice go
to waste. I loved how I'd felt when
I mastered the keepy-uppies. It had
given me a real sense of achievement.
I might not have had the chance to
show them to my teamies but the main
thing was I'd proved to myself that I
wasn't a complete klutz with a ball.

In the end that's all that matters,
isn't it? How you feel about yourself?
I felt more self-confident and heaps
fitter. I didn't want to let that go.
Smart girls exercise. Fact.

Hey, and guess what else happened?
When I went back inside everyone was
signing the T-shirts. Someone grabbed
me and shoved a felt pen under my
nose and said, "Amy! Sign here! Sign
here!" Even JJ wanted my signature.

"Put 'babe' after it or I won't
know it's you," she said. LOL!

Mandy even got everyone to
customize one of the spare T-shirts,
and she's having it framed and put
above the bar, so I get a kind of
legacy after all. And in clothing.
How appropriate!

Don't go away now. Some of us might

have left the building but Megan,
JJ, Petra, Tabinda, Daisy and Dylan
are still in the picture. In fact,
Megan is busy this second getting a
new team together before next season
starts. You have soooooooooooo got to
stick around for that.

Buh-bye, girlfriends. It's been
fab.

Amy xxxxxx

WANTED

Girls aged 8–11 to join
awesome football team the
Parrs Under 11s (winners of this
year's Nettie Honeyball Cup)

Training every Tuesday at
Lornton FC ground

Fun Open Day will be held on
Saturday 7 June at Lornton FC

Email slewisparrsfc@gmail.com